Della Dimmitt

A Story of Madeira

Della Dimmitt

A Story of Madeira

ISBN/EAN: 9783337771621

Printed in Europe, USA, Canada, Australia, Japan

Cover: Foto ©Andreas Hilbeck / pixelio.de

More available books at **www.hansebooks.com**

A

STORY OF MADEIRA

BY

DELLA DIMMITT

CINCINNATI: CURTS & JENNINGS
NEW YORK: EATON & MAINS
1896

CONTENTS.

ILLUSTRATIONS.

A STORY OF MADEIRA.

A STORY OF MADEIRA.

Chapter I.

AN ACT OF PROVIDENCE.

IN the North Atlantic, some five hundred miles southwest of Lisbon, and near four hundred miles due west of Morocco, lies the island of Madeira. Its discovery, in 1419, was the second achievement of the early Portuguese mariners, who have left their names and their history in a wide track upon the map of the world. At that time, John the Great was king of Portugal, and Prince Henry, the third of his illustrious sons, after distinguishing himself in a campaign against the Moors, in which he and his four brothers led the flower of the young Portuguese chivalry, had taken up his residence in ancient Sagre, and was devoting his wealth and energies to the promotion of a notable cause.

Until then the rich products of the Orient were carried overland to Venice, the distributing point of all Europe. It was the great hope of Prince Henry, "the Navigator," to discover a southern water-route to India, which, by one bold, brilliant stroke, would add to the glory of Portugal, deprive the Venetians of their commercial prestige, and turn the current of trade toward Lisbon, where his father loved to dwell and watch the white sails pass to and fro along the Tagus. All the adventurous spirits of the kingdom gathered around Prince Henry, and while he never commanded the expeditions in person, he was universally acknowledged to be the guiding genius of them all.

This was but the beginning of that
marvelous expansion of power which has
given Portugal a story among the nations
of earth—a story as eventful, as picturesque, as glorious as even her prouder
Castilian neighbor can tell. And when
it is remembered that these sea-faring
men put out on unknown seas in such
crazy crafts as a sailor of to-day would
hardly trust outside of the land's sight,
and that there was at that time none of
the modern knowledge of the tides and
winds, their successful ventures seem all
the more wonderful.

Prince Henry hailed with delight the
news of the discovery of Madeira, so
called because of its wooded appearance.
The island was soon colonized, and the
prince himself introduced the culture of
sugar-cane and the grapevine, which
have since been the chief source of its
wealth.

Soon after its colonization a terrible fire broke out, which burned steadily for seven years, destroying much of the natural beauty of the island, and for a time threatening the destruction of the little colony; but, like all other things Portuguese, it had strange tenacity of life, and grew to share the fortunes and misfortunes of the mother country.

In a little cup-shaped depression among encircling mountains, Funchal, the island's capital and largest city, has been built. It looks seaward on the south, and some half-mile out, on a natural defense of rocks, is the old fort, commanding the entrance to the Bay of Funchal. A massive stone wall, sixteen feet in thickness, and rising fourteen feet above the sea-level, curves inward from the fort and joins the island, making a safe entrance where, in former times, the short and choppy waves were a constant men-

HARBOR OF FUNCHAL.

ace to vessels making the pass between the fort and the harbor.

A broad, clean beach of white stones skirts the bay, and a wide street, paved with the same clean stones, leads directly into the city, which stretches away up the gently-sloping mountain-sides for some three miles in as many directions. A few half-ruined archways yet remain that once broke the solid length of a stone wall inclosing the city, and adding its picturesque touch of the olden times. It is a "white city," the dwellings being built almost entirely of native stone, with red-tiled roofs and wide verandas, showing glimpses of cool, dim interiors through the overhanging masses of vines. Well-kept parks break the monotonous length of streets solidly built up of business and dwelling houses, the most beautiful of them all being the central park that is at the crossing of the

two main thoroughfares and near the
heart of the city. Fountains, flowers in
rank luxuriance, clean, pebbly walks, rus-
tic seats, and a quaint band-stand, in
which a band plays two evenings of every
week, make it a delightful resort of the
people. A cathedral rises off to the side
of the park, and from its tall tower sweet-
toned bells sound the hours.

Half-way up the mountain-side, and
beyond the ruined archways that mark
the limits of the city, is one of the smaller
Roman Catholic churches, called " Our
Lady of the Mount," interesting because
of the magnificent view it affords of the
city down in the valley, and of the ex-
panse of blue waters, with that peculiar
wall-like effect the unobstructed breakers
give as they pile up far out at sea.

Beyond the mountains stretches the
open country, almost the whole of it en-
tailed estates of the nobility, but divided

into small holdings, given over to the peasants for cultivation, the lines of survey marked by stone walls or box hedges, and not infrequently by solid banks of nothing but fuchsias in full bloom. Quaint little peasant cottages, with high thatched roofs, meet the eye as the traveler swings through the country, carried in a hammock suspended from the shoulders of two strong carriers, or is borne more luxuriously in a cushioned and silk-curtained palanquin; for beasts of burden are rare and expensive in the island.

It has a semi-tropical climate, and from the harbor at Funchal, where the white-winged vessels come and go, cargoes of tropical fruits and casks of wine of the famous "Old Madeira" vintage, are sent to the markets of the world.

And this is Madeira, this little island only eighteen miles wide by fifty-four miles long—the "old country" that its wandering sons will tell you about with misty eyes and a wistfulness of voice that speaks to you of something loftier than the mountains and deeper than the sea of their own Madeira.

In 1838, Robert Reid Kalley, a native of Scotland and a physician from Edinburgh, who had felt himself especially called to the work of a missionary, was on his way to his appointed field. He had been ordained by the Free Church of Scotland, and appointed to a mission in China; but while on the way his wife sickened, and it became apparent that she could not endure the strain of the long, hard voyage. At last the doctor requested the captain to put them off at the nearest port. It was one of those moments when a man walks blindly as he follows after faith.

It chanced that the little island of Madeira was the point of land first

reached; but in the light of after history, there can be no question that "Al-
mighty God that chance did guide."
Landed—stranded, as it were—in this
foreign country, and unacquainted with
its language, the doctor accepted it as
one of the inscrutable providences, and
prepared to take up his residence among
a strange people. He began at once a
study of the language, and sought to
enter into the life around him with the
easy adaptability of the truly called missionary.

Dr. Kalley was a man cast in a grand
mold. Strongly built and of commanding stature, there was a fine dignity in
his bearing which made him a conspicuous and kingly figure wherever he stood
among men. His face was that of a true
Scot, resolute, strong, and open as the
day; but there was that same expression,
a sort of spiritual illumination, in the

keen, clear blue eyes, that shines—yea,
speaks—in the eyes of men who live very
close to God, and who love their fellow-
men with a deep, unspeakable, and self-
abnegating love. He inspired confidence
in others, while the most of us must win
it slowly, proving ourselves worthy before the precious thing is given, and his
medical skill furnished him the means of
immediate and direct contact with the
people.

Madeira had never been occupied as a
mission field, and, having no authority
from the Church with which he had been
identified in Edinburgh, Dr. Kalley resolved upon opening up a work upon entirely independent lines. He was a man
of great wealth, and in his act of consecration to his calling, had not forgotten
to add his treasure to the list of taxable
property, which included himself with all
his varied talents and youthful ambition ;

for he was at this time but twenty-nine years of age.

Like a practical Scotchman, Dr. Kalley entered upon his self-appointed mission by ministering to the physical needs of the people. He opened a hospital and dispensary in Funchal, and gave medical treatment, free of charge, to all who came to him. The hold this course gave him upon the people was necessarily very great.

The native physicians were ill-taught, bungling practitioners, and the majority of the people were very poor. The reasons for this general condition of poverty were obvious. The population was over large for the size of the island, and the holding of the land by the gentry drew the distinctions of class sharply, and increased the difficulty for the common people to gain a living.

In the country day-laborers received

their board and but ten cents a day additional; and even the wages of skilled mechanics in the city never exceeded eighty cents a day. However, as an offset to these hard conditions, the mild climate, never approaching the severity of a northern winter, and the abundance of fruits, reduced the necessities of life to the smallest limits.

In dispensing his charities, Dr. Kalley insisted upon but one condition, and that was for all who wished a consultation to present themselves at his office by nine o'clock in the morning. When all were assembled, he would read a chapter from the Bible, point the people to the Great Physician, and offer up a simple, earnest prayer for the effectiveness of the remedies he was about to administer, and pleaded that their infirmities of soul might also yield to the touch of the divine healing.

Schools were next established by the doctor in various parts of the island, he himself hiring the teachers and furnishing the text-books. It was an unprecedented offer; for Madeira had never maintained any system of free schools, and the great majority of the people could neither read nor write. It had long been the custom with the more prosperous families to send the eldest child to some one of the parochial schools in the city, and in turn the younger children learned of that more highly-favored one; but no such advantages as these were to be had by any except the richer few. The heavy shadow of Romanism lay upon the entire island, and the deplorable mental and spiritual darkness was fully equal to that of all ancient or modern countries belonging distinctively to the Roman Catholic faith.

The inhabitants of Madeira showed

their appreciation of the Scotchman's offer by the very best way in their power—they flocked to the schools from all directions, and it is on record that at one time there were eight hundred adults in attendance, and some twenty-five hundred at various times. The sessions were held by night, at "early candle-light," so that the regular working hours might not be infringed upon.

The Bible was one of the text-books in use, and these copies were the first ones ever seen in Madeira, with the exeption of a consignment of eighty volumes, sent for the use of the priests some years before, at the express command of the Queen of Portugal.

The people were teachable, and, rarer still, were grateful. There was no such popular man in all the length and breadth of the island as Dr. Kalley. He was everybody's friend. The fame of his cures spread abroad, and even the exclusive and wealthy sought relief at his hand. The municipal authorities of Funchal tendered him a formal vote of thanks for what they delighted to term his "disinterested acts of benevolence and philanthropy in the establishment of free schools, hospitals, and dispensaries in different parts of the island."

It is pleasant to dwell upon these earlier years of Dr. Kalley's ministry in Madeira, when popular favor was his. His coming in the character of a public benefactor calls to one's memory a curious story interwoven with the history of Portugal concerning the last ruler of the powerful house of Aviz.

The blood of the English Plantagenets was united with the illegitimate blood of the great John, founder of the house, which in its course produced some right royal kings. The last of the race was

Dom Sebastian, a fair-haired, blue-eyed boy, who was declared of age, and given the right to rule over Portugal when only in his fifteenth year. From the Hapsburg strain he had inherited a certain German dreaminess, which, commingling with the Spanish fanaticism, made him a Crusader, though the crusade spirit itself had died away throughout Europe long before his time.

Filled with the dream of becoming a brave "Soldier of the Cross," he taxed the last resources of an already decaying country to furnish means and men for an expedition against the Moors, the object of which was the recovery of some worthless towns along the barren African coast, which his grandfather, John III, had voluntarily abandoned to the Mohammedans. With the largest fleet at his command, numbers of Spanish and German mercenaries, and ten thousand

Portuguese soldiers, young and, like their king, bent on adventure, he set sail for Morocco. The Pope blessed the enterprise, and sent him an arrow of Saint Sebastian; but the fortunes of war were not to be commanded by the infallible one's blessing, or even by the arrow of a saint. From first to last the enterprise was a failure, and though Dom Sebastian fought like a brave, true knight, he led a forlorn hope.

It was on the 4th of August, 1578, at daybreak, when the decisive battle was on, and before night nine thousand soldiers lay dead on the field, and the rest were taken prisoners, except a body of fifty horsemen surrounding the person of their king. An equerry flung up a flag of truce, and was in the act of making a formal surrender, when the impetuous young king, who bore this device upon his sword, "In noble death lies life's

3

whole honor," broke away from his
guard and dashed single-handed upon
the Moorish cavalry. Angry at the
breach of faith, the Moors instantly cut
him down, and the last romantic figure
of the Portuguese Crusaders had vanished
forever.

For some unaccountable cause, the
Portuguese of the lower classes did not
believe Dom Sebastian dead. The circumstances of his romantic expedition
among the Moors had strangely fired the
popular imagination, and, believing the
protection of Heaven especially vouch-
safed to him, they looked for Dom Sebastian to appear among them again.
The idea embodied itself into a religious
faith, and a powerful sect sprang up, calling themselves Sebastianistai, and looking always toward the coming of the
" Principe Encuberto," or Hidden Prince.
Though more than three hundred years

have elapsed, and no less than five im-
postors have been put to ignominious
death for proclaiming themselves Dom
Sebastians, and asserting claims to the
throne of Portugal, the superstition still
clings to the more ignorant Portuguese,
and in every great national stress they
have looked with a great longing for the
coming of the true Dom Sebastian, who
would bring them deliverance in war and
wise rule in peace.

Another nation once looked through
long centuries of waiting toward the coming of a great " Hidden Prince " indeed.
And the world is always looking, in one
way and another, for the rising of some
wiser ruler than has hitherto borne rule
over it, some great dispenser of bounties,
whose far-reaching humanity will touch
even to the confines of a single human
life.   And in the course of years a prince

does sometimes stand revealed among men, for the Record tells us that once at least, "there was a man sent from God." There are still men sent from God, and one had come to Madeira.

Chapter II.

PERSECUTIONS BEGUN.

A S time passed on, the real object of Dr. Kalley's work became apparent. It was for the salvation of the people he had been moved to these "acts of disinterested benevolence." He had given the islanders an open Bible, and, believing with Luther, that it is its own best interpreter, he had quietly waited until the Book had proven itself the "Sword of the Spirit."

They read it with increasing delight and wonder, this new Book, which so simply unfolded the way of life to the true believer. There was nothing in it of priestly intercession, or of the ancient customs and stately ceremonial of the Romish Church. They marveled at that.

The priests, having to meet so many questions concerning the very foundations of the ancient faith, finally became alarmed for the safety of the Church, and to stay the rising spirit of inquiry, the bishop officially declared this new Bible was "a book from hell."

Dr. Kalley met them on their own ground, and caused certified comparisons of the Bible he had introduced among them, and the version which had received the sanction of the Queen of Portugal, to be posted in conspicuous places. Verse by verse they were found to be identical. In the face of such indisputable evidence, the bishop went further, and pronounced a curse upon the Bible and all who should read it, and gave warning to the teachers, whom Dr. Kalley had employed, to discontinue their teaching at the risk of imprisonment.

In the city of Funchal there were

many English-speaking people. The official residence of the English consul was there, and the well-known healthfulness of Madeira had drawn great numbers of invalids to winter in the mild climate of the island. A Scottish Church of the Protestant faith had been erected for the use of these foreigners, and they were protected by certain provisions in the treaty between the two nations in the free excrcise of their religion.

It was some four years after his arrival that Dr. Kalley had commenced to hold regular religious services for the natives. These meetings were usually held in the open air, often on the mountainside, and the doctor preached to them there; or in his absence, some one of the newly taught read selections from the Scriptures. And so eager were the people to hear that they came walking over the mountains for great distances, and

from all directions, gathering in great
crowds to feed upon the Word of Life
as it fell from the lips of their beloved
physician, teacher, and friend.

One Sabbath morning two Portuguese,
who had been moved to make a public
renunciation of the ancient faith, came to
the little Scottish Church and partook of
the communion. This was sufficient pre-
text for the priests to combine against
the great popular movement led on by Dr.
Kalley. The two believers were at once
excommunicated, and from that time on
the spirit of persecution was abroad in
the land.

The schools were broken up with violence, the teachers imprisoned, and threats
made against the life of Dr. Kalley. In
defiance of the treaty, he was at last
seized, tried, and thrown into prison under
an old law of the Inquisition which had
not been in force for more than two hun-

STREET VIEW IN FUNCHAL.

dred years. At the expiration of five months he was released; but the new governor, who had recently received his appointment over the island, openly declared his intention of driving the doctor from Madeira, and thus putting an end to the work.

About this time, Dr. Kalley withdrew from the island for a brief period, visiting friends in Scotland, and afterward living quietly in Lisbon, in the hope that the storm would expend its force.

During his absence, Mr. Hewitson, a young minister from Edinburgh, was ordained by the Free Church of Scotland, and sent as missionary to Madeira. He it was who first organized the converts into a Church belonging to this communion. It is the universal testimony of all who remember this devoted young minister that he was so unreservedly given up to the service of the Master

that when he preached it seemed as if
the very heavens drew near and opened
before the eyes of the people. He frequently said that he knew Christ better
than he knew any other being, and it was
always that thought of the personal relation between God and man which was
the keynote in the character of this pure
young spirit, and formed the burden of
his message to men.

Upon Dr. Kalley's return to Madeira,
the persecutions broke out afresh. A Jesuit upon the island, following out the dis- .
tinctive methods of that notorious order,
gave form to the growing spirit of opposition to the missionary and his converts
by banding the priests together in a se-
cret organization. They subverted the
press of the island to their use, and
through its agency openly advocated murder, imprisonment, and beating for the
Bible-readers.

The civil authority was tacitly committed to the work of exterminating the new faith, and the persecutions began in earnest. One woman was tried and condemned to death because she persisted in affirming that the wafer in the hands of a priest was not the real body of Christ. The formal setting forth of her offense and sentence is a curious instrument to be found in court records of our own day. The sentence, however, was never executed; for the friends of the condemned woman appealed to a superior tribunal in Portugal, which approved of the grounds of the sentence, but reversed it on some minor technicality. She suffered a long imprisonment, and but for the persistent effort of friends would no doubt have suffered death also.

From the lips of the survivors of those perilous times of fifty years ago comes the story—the latest chapter of the Inquisition continued into the nineteenth century.

One of them, for many years an elder in the Presbyterian Church here in our own country, was a pupil in one of the night-schools in the rural districts. He had never seen a printed page until he entered the school; but after the teacher employed by Dr. Kalley had been forbidden to teach longer, he was one of the advanced pupils selected to carry on the work.

They met at nightfall in the mountains, and for a number of months eluded the vigilance of the officers; but at last the young teacher, together with his father, four brothers, sixteen other men, and five converted women, were arrested and taken to the Funchal jail. They were kept in close confinement for two entire years, and during all that time the jail-keeper was forbidden to give food to

these twenty-two men and five women,
whose only offense was that of reading
and believing the Scriptures, though
those confined with them, who were
guilty of overt acts against the civil law,
were abundantly supplied with food.
These sufferers for the truth's sake were
fed by the bounty of friends and sympa-
thizers outside.

The first serious difficulty occurred
when all were required to attend mass in
the jail, and these twenty-two men refused to kneel in presence of the "host."
They were then beaten, one of them so
severely that at the time of his death, two
years ago, he still bore upon his person
the scars left by the lash; but not one of
the number yielded, though their outward
observance of the form would have saved
them any further difficulty. At the expiration of the two years they were al-
lowed a trial, and were released, but were

threatened with immediate rearrest and the full penalty of law if they did not return to the communion of the Roman Catholic Church. They fled to the mountains, and for the time found safety among the natural fastnesses, together with scores of other unfortunate ones driven from their homes.

The lawyer who defended the prisoners was afterward compelled to flee for refuge to Portugal. The people were so incensed at him for undertaking the cause of Bible-readers, they would not tolerate his presence in Madeira.

There were now seizures daily, and trials in which none of the Bible-readers, as they were derisively called, could expect justice. False witnesses were often hired; the accused one was required to pay the costs of his own trial, and for his maintenance while in jail. They were excommunicated, and with that sentence

went the command to all loyal Romanists: "Let none give them fire, water,
bread, or anything that may be necessary
to them for their support. Let none pay
them their debts." And this command
was so literally carried out that none of
those who had property were able to sell
at any price. Some few made arrange-
ments with friends to hold in trust for
them what they had; but the sentence
of excommunication practically reduced
every one of the early believers to
poverty.

The story of a man yet living, as he
relates it, holds the clearest reflection of
the stealthy, pursuing power of the Church
of Rome over one who renounces allegiance to the ancient faith; though, in
point of fact, the occurrence was a number of years after the violence of the persecutions had subsided, and after the earlier converts had left the island.

The narrator was the son of a wine-
grower in the diocese of St. Anthony,
about four miles out of Funchal. As evidence of the mental darkness of the people, he says that, of his father's family
·and immediate connection, twenty in all,
not one could read. Upon the opening
of Dr. Kalley's school, this boy became a
pupil, and afterward, though but eleven
years of age, taught from house to house,
and wrote letters for those of the Protestants who had friends in the faith elsewhere. He added, by way of apology,
that in Madeira they have a proverb
which says, "In the land of the blind, he
that hath an eye may be king."

The study of the Bible became the
boy's absorbing passion, as, indeed, it was
with all who first came to look upon its
inspired pages; but the order had long
gone out through the island that all
copies of the Bible should be seized and

destroyed. Hundreds of volumes were, in the course of time, taken from the people, and there are many incidents related of the ways in which some of the more fortunate ones succeeded in saving their precious copies, secreting them in the thick foliage of trees, or among the easily-loosened stones of the walls surrounding the yards. This family had been able to retain their Bible by placing it in a hollow place in the ceiling. The house had been searched many times, and the daughter of the landlord, a young woman who was a most devout Roman Catholic, had asked again and again what they had done with "that black book."

In their reverence for the Bible as the inspired of the Spirit, they felt no reproach in openly declaring they had no "black book;" but towards evening the Bible would be drawn from its hiding-place, and, holding it between him and the uncertain light of the fireplace, with his back to the window, concealing it from the view of any chance passer-by, the boy would read aloud to the assembled family. But one day the door was suddenly flung open, and the landlord's daughter ran up to him, saying, with a mocking laugh, "Ah! I have the black book at last."

It was a sore trial to them all; but the boy at once wrote a letter to Dr. Miller, the brother-in-law of Dr. Kalley, then absent in London, describing the manner of the Bible's capture, and asking for another. He lost the letter while on his way to mail it in Funchal. It was found and taken to the priest of St. Anthony parish, who read it publicly, and admonished all who had dealings with the boy's father neither to buy nor sell to him. Of course, that meant starvation, which was a serious matter for a man with a helpless family dependent upon him, and, after consulting with his wife, they decided to send the boy to confessional. Much against his will, he presented himself before the priest, but, upon refusing to kneel before his confessor, was roughly seized by the shoulder, and forced into the main audience-room. It was during Lent, and the room was full, and in presence of them all the priest related the scene in the confessional, and after another ineffectual attempt to compel the boy to kneel and answer according to the spirit of one who desires absolution at the hands of a priest, he was excommunicated then and there, and flung into the street, cursed as a dog and a devil, which is the height of profanity in Madeira.

Not long after this occurrence, while working with his brothers in the pine woods, the boy mashed his thumb. No part of his hand was injured except the end of his thumb just above the first joint; for he distinctly remembers crushing his handkerchief in the wounded hand to dry his tears. They were nine miles from home, but they walked back as hurriedly as possible, and the father started with his son to consult a surgeon of Funchal.

In passing the church of St. Anthony, they saw the priest on the balcony, who inquired the cause of their journey.

"Ah, it is too bad," he said, in a kindly tone, after hearing the account of the accident; "such a promising boy, too. Where will you take him for treatment?"

"I don't know yet," answered the father.

"Well, then," said the priest—the same one who had excommunicated and cursed him a few weeks before—"I advise you to take him to the city hospital. He will be treated there free of charge, and I myself will give you a certificate of admission for him."

The father, who could not read at all, gladly received the paper, and, upon reaching the hospital and presenting the certificate, was told that the thumb would require some three weeks' treatment, and that he might as well go home and leave his son, that he would be well cared for.

In the afternoon the superintendent of the hospital came to the boy, and said with rather a baleful inflection of tone:

"You will never write again for the Protestants, you—you Calvinist boy!"

In that moment it flashed upon him that he was to be the victim of some pre-arranged plan; but he looked up calmly into the superintendent's face, and said:

"I know I am in your power; but remember you will have to meet me at the judgment bar, and answer for what you do to me to-day."

A bell rang, and the medical students came hurrying into the clinic. They seized the boy and held him down on the operating-table in spite of his screams and struggles. He was soon under the influence of a powerful opiate, and next remembers the touch of a gentle hand on his forehead, and the voice of one of the physicians, himself an irreligious man, saying:

"O poor boy! poor boy! draw thy maimed arm to thyself."

He looked down, and his hand was severed at the wrist, and his first words spoken through tears were these:

"I can never write again."

The father, coming next day to see his son, was heart-broken to find what had been done, and summoning Dr. Miller, who was again in Funchal, they visited the morgue together. The doctor examined the severed hand, and found it

articulated perfectly; but the records of
the hospital disclosed the certificate of admission, which read thus: "This is that
Calvinist pest—fix him."

Among the early believers was a man
by the name of Martin. One night he
was quietly walking home from one of
Dr. Kalley's meetings, when he was suddenly overpowered by a number of men
who lay in wait for him along the unfre-
quented way. They beat him severely,
and then dragged him alongside one of
the stone walls that skirted the fields.
One after another the men climbed upon
the wall, and jumped from it down upon
the prostrate body of the Bible-reader.
The blood gushed from his wounds, and
they left him for dead. Recovering con-
sciousness, he raised his head and feebly
asked of the passers-by a drink of water
from the small stream that ran near at
hand, and there was not one moved by the

commonest humanity to do this simple act of service for a dying fellow-man. He was afterward buried at a cross-road, the common place of interment for heretics, as was also Antonio Reis, the wealthiest man of his locality, an elder in the Church, and one of the early converts.

And when it is remembered that all Roman Catholic people are intensely superstitious, and that the cross-roads were popularly supposed to be the meeting-place of uneasy ghosts, witches, and devils, it was a most uncanny place in which to lie, with the passers-by treading over one by day, and the evil spirits holding high carnival by night.

As the strength of the persecutions waxed greater, the believers were drawn together in a closer bond of fellowship. Frequent meetings were held for the strengthening of their faith, and among the places open for these services was

PARK AND OPERA-HOUSE, FUNCHAL.

the home of three English sisters, the Misses Rutherford. They lived in the "Quinta das Augustias," a beautiful residence of some twenty or thirty rooms, with wide verandas encircling the house, which was set in the midst of finely-kept grounds.

One Sabbath morning a little company assembled to listen to the reading of the Bible and to hear a letter addressed to his flock by the young pastor, Mr. Hewitson, who had before this time returned to Scotland. Before the hour's service had closed, a mob, composed of the worst element in Funchal, led on by the Jesuits, surrounded the house. Their howls and curses resounded through all that long, dreadful day and night, and stones frequently came crashing through the windows, while the frightened inmates lay concealed in a remote corner of the house.

After midnight the mob forced an en-

trance, beat one of the servants into
insensibility, and with flaring torches
made the circuit of the house, only to
find some dozen or more defenseless
women clinging to one another in helpless terror.   With renewed threats of
violence in case the meetings were not
discontinued, the mob at last retired,
leaving one of the Rutherford ladies,
who was an invalid, to die from the shock
before another week expired.

Among the believers, who had fre-
quented these meetings at the home of
the English women, was a mother and
her two young daughters.   Her husband
had not renounced Romanism, though secretly sympathizing with the new movement, and in some clandestine way he became aware that his wife and daughters
were in danger.   Together with a friend,
a merchant of Funchal, he arranged a
plan for their safety.

One at a time they walked down to the beach dressed in their common, every-day attire, as if they had gone to join the company of bathers. It was in the early evening, and, unnoticed by the crowd, one by one they were led away by the merchant and secreted in his house. There were five of them in all—the mother, two grown daughters, a boy of eleven, and a child not yet two years old. They were in hiding some seven days before their place of concealment was suspected. Some Romanists then came to the merchant, saying, "We intend to search your house."

"All right," said the merchant, with apparent frankuess; "come ahead; but you will find no one there."

In great haste he sent a laborer from his plantation, miles away in the country, to remove the family. They started at nine o'clock at night, and near morning reached a disused cow-shed, where they concealed themselves under a great pile of bean-straw.

In the meantime, Mr. Martin had been murdered, and there were evidences of a well-formed plan for the murder of Dr. Kalley. The doctor had resisted all entreaties of his friends to flee, saying it was his duty to remain and comfort his sorrowing people. They had reviewed the situation, and, after much serious thought, had at length resolved to leave the island. Dr. Kalley had repeatedly said to them, by way of comfort, "The ships will come for you—the ships will come for you."

During the week that followed the mobbing of the Rutherford house, Dr. Kalley wrote to the governor of Madeira, clearly setting forth his danger; and in answer, the Romanist governor said that the British residents upon the island were looked upon with "mistrust and disgust," and that the disturbance was only "the fruit of the tree Dr. Kalley had planted on the island, and it could produce nothing but discord and trouble."

The doctor next addressd the English consul, inclosing an anonymous letter he had only that day received; and in which a full and, as it afterward appeared, a true outline of the next day's plan of action was given; but from that source he received no promise of protection.

The only thing remaining to be done was to barricade his residence and prepare to defend his own life as best he could. Procuring bolts and bars, with the help of servants, he made the place as secure as possible, and at two o'clock the next morning was accompanying a friend, who had spent the night with him, to the outer gate. They found the gate slightly ajar; and standing in its shadow, overheard some masked men speak of "the killing on the morrow." One of the men was busily sharpening a large knife, and another was urging him to enter at once. As there had been a guard of soldiers stationed in front of the house early Saturday evening, ostensibly for the protection of the missionary's household, and this discussion of plans had taken place in their presence, it was evident that the guard were traitors.

Hastily pushing the gate shut, the doctor and his friend returned to the house, and after a prayer for Divine help in this moment of sore distress, the doctor made his escape through the rear of the house in the disguise of a peasant. He climbed over the low stone wall surrounding the spacious grounds, and, creeping along in its shadow—for it was a clear, moonlight night, almost as light as day—he succeeded in eluding the vigilance of both guard and mob, and made his way to the "Pinheiros," the home of his brother-in-law, Dr. Miller.

A signal was at once hoisted from the house, and the anxious watchers of the doctor's household knew that, for a time at least, he was safe. Stealthily, one by one, the remaining members of the family followed along the same track, and were hidden in the "Pinheiros." Morning broke; it was the Sabbath, and but one week since the mobbing of the Rutherford place.

The mother and her four children had, by this time, returned to their first place of concealment in the merchant's home. The house had been built after a favorite fashion in Madeira, with one of the ground-floor rooms supporting a succession of rooms, rising one above another. The roof of this tower-like addition commanded a glorious view of the ocean

and of the mountains in the back-
ground. In the room just beneath this
observatory were the refugees, and one of
the surviving daughters tells the story of
that eventful Sunday morning, her black
eyes flashing with a vision of the strange
sight they saw more than a half-century
ago. It was a very still day, and they
could distinctly hear the bells in the cathedral tower striking the time of day.
There were bells of varying sizes,—a
small one to strike every fifteen min-
utes, a larger one for the half hours,
and the largest of all for the hours.

When eleven o'clock came, the large
bell struck just once, and before it had
time to strike again, a rocket went up
in the air; then another exploded in
quick succession ; and, in the flash of an
eye, from the cathedral, from behind trees
and walls, from everywhere, there came
pouring out men dressed entirely in

white—white trousers, white coats, white shirts, and white hats. It was not a costume of Madeira—such a sight had never been seen before—but it was a preconcerted sign by which the Romanists were to know one another.

The men turned, and swept up the street toward Dr. Kalley's place, never doubting that he was inside; but at that very moment he was taken out of the "Pinheiros" in a hammock, disguised in woman's attire, and, covered over with a linen sheet, was being hurried down to the shore by two bearers. And O, the prayers that followed him!

At first one of the bearers refused to carry the hammock without knowing who was inside of it; but the impression prevailed that it was a sick English lady being carried to board an English steamer then lying at anchor in the harbor, and he was persuaded to go on. The crowd had

5

now broken into Dr. Kalley's house, and, after searching through every part of it and finding their prey gone, they had taken his library—ten thousand dollars' worth of books—and his valuable surgical instruments, into the street. They beat them with sticks, and there set fire to them; and while the fire was burning, it was noised abroad that the missionary had escaped.

One of the bearers, perhaps having a strong suspicion that all was not as he was led to believe, drew a corner of the sheet aside; but Dr. Kalley's friend, who walked beside the hammock, rearranged the covering and they proceeded again. Finally the same bearer declared he could go no further, that "it was hell for him;" but again his suspicions were quieted, and they went on. Three several times they stopped, and as many times were persuaded to continue. At last the shore was reached, the hammock was placed

in a boat, and they rapidly pushed out
to sea.

Then the men came from the vain
search, and in an instant the whole bay
was alive with little boats, manned by
the men in white.

Dr. Kalley's boat pulled alongside the
steamer, and he was quickly taken aboard,
still in the hammock. The men came
close to the vessel's side, and demanded
of the captain whether or not the missionary was on board. The captain tried
to allay their suspicions; but seeing they
were bent on an unequivocal answer, he
went below, and told Dr. Kalley he had
better allow himself to be seen; and pres-
ently the doctor came on deck, leaning on
the captain's arm. He knew he was safe.
A brave man commanded the English
ship, and above them, bold and high,
floated the Union Jack!

For one moment there was intense

stillness, as the missionary drew himself up to his full, splendid height, and fearlessly stood before them. Then such a prolonged howl of rage burst from the throats of those baffled men that it is said the sound of it, reaching shore, was like the sound of the ocean as the wind roars over it in a winter's storm.

There was nothing left to do but wreak their vengeance on the senseless objects in Dr. Kalley's house. So they returned to shore, broke every pane of window-glass in the house, destroyed every article of furniture, and sent cobble-stones crashing into the house until, it is said, they lay as thick on the floor as they lay outside in the street. Other houses of the converts were visited and despoiled in the same manner.

One woman tells of concealing herself in the thick foliage of a grape-arbor; but the outcry of a little child, hiding with her, discovered them to a party of the mob. She was dragged from among the vines, and struck in the face by one of the men.

All this time the consul was inactive. He had laid aside his consular dress, and had caused the English flag to be taken down from above the consular residence; and a consul in a "sailor's round jacket," who walked about amidst the mob and viewed its depredations, did not inspire that wholesome awe which might have been expected in a Portuguese mob in presence of Her British Majesty's official representative.

The governor, who had all the forces of the island at his command, refused to allow them to interfere; though, to their honor it is said, there were both military and civil officers of the Government who pleaded for permission to stay the violence of the conspirators. Colonel Taxeiro, commander of the Funchal garrison, who wished to disperse them, but was forbidden to do so by the governor, determined to act independently of all orders from him in case other riots should occur. This was not that these officials sympathized with the religious faith of Dr. Kalley and his followers, but rather that they deprecated lawless violence, and had all the soldier's high regard for the law of the land and the dignity of human life and personal liberty.

Later, England demanded and obtained full indemnity for Dr. Kalley's pecuniary losses, and the Queen of Portugal was forced into dismissing the governor and instituting an official inquiry; though that was but a farce, after all, resulting in the acquittal of all concerned in the operations of the mob.

There is but one conclusion, and that is, there was collusion between the ecclesiastical and the civil powers in thus violating the courtesy of nations, and setting aside the sacred obligations of a treaty.

And, too, this story of wrong and violence done to a law-abiding British subject, a philanthropist in the very broadest sense of that word, and to scores of inoffensive men and women, who suffered in the same spirit of patience as the earlier martyrs had done, who never gave railing for railing, and who asked for nothing more than the privilege of worshiping God in sincere and simple fashion,—offers most incontrovertible, and damaging testimony against the broad toleration which the Roman Catholics affect in our own tolerant country.

Here is no tale of the Dark Ages, when the lawless times and the fiercer temper of men pleaded in their own excuse; but as history of the very middle of our pres-

ent century, it is most clear and indisputable evidence of the unchangeable
spirit of Romanism, that yet dreams of
dominating the world by the power of
soft persuasion or the exterminating
sword, as the times allow.

Chapter III.

ESCAPE OF THE CONVERTS.

THE two weeks following the escape of Dr. Kalley were weeks of trial to the pursued and persecuted people. They fled to the mountains, to the thickets, or wherever retreat offered, in many instances leaving their homes in flames and their worldly possessions to the destruction of their Roman Catholic neighbors.

There was no protection for them anywhere in the island; but out in the bay there lay at anchor an English merchant-vessel and some men-of-war. These men-of-war fired their guns by way of a sign to the hunted creatures that, though their own Government might refuse them its defense, there was at least safety on board an English ship. A consular reprimand was given, but it was unnoticed; and at intervals, through all those fourteen dreadful days and nights, there still came across the quiet waters of the bay that friendly, steady voice of English guns—those short, sharp volleys, that everywhere, in all waters, denoted the presence of English strength.

Secretly, by night, the people made their way to the shore, and were taken on board the merchantman, the *William of Glasgow.*

There are scores of men and women yet living who recall, as if it had been but yesterday, the incidents of those crowded days that impressed themselves upon their childish minds. One woman, then a child of eight years, remembers her father nightly guarding his dwelling, while the mother, with two little girls clinging to her skirts and her baby in her arms, made her way painfully through the pine-thickets, a half-mile from the house, to sleep upon the bare ground, under the open sky.

They were among the first to take refuge in the *William of Glasgow*. It was at one o'clock in the morning when they made their way down to the beach, and were taken out to the vessel in one of the small boats. The little craft was so heavily freighted that they narrowly escaped drowning.

"And my mother was always so timid of the water," continues my narrator. "Why, she never could be persuaded even to stand on the beach and watch the waves; but that night she clasped my little brother close in her arms, and with my little sister and me clinging hold of her, she sang, O so loud and clear!"

And she sang the song for me in her native tongue—sang it through gathering tears—a wild, sweet melody, with a tri-

umphant note running through it, that
I could well fancy rising high above the
splash of the waves, the heavy straining
of the oars, and even above a weak woman's fears.

There was sad breaking of home-ties
in many instances. The mother, who,
with her four children, had been given a
refuge in the merchant's home, parted
from her husband, not to see him again
for three long years, and then, after a
brief reunion, she left him lying in a
South American burying-ground, while
she went on alone to find a home in another and strange continent.

There was romance, too. A young
girl, who was the only convert out of her
family, left home in the night to join her
betrothed, and marry him on shipboard.
Before leaving, she stole through the familiar rooms of her birthplace, and, in
spirit, bade farewell to her mother and

the other members of the family, as they were asleep. She is an old woman now, and has never looked upon their faces since that night.

On the 23d of August, 1846, the vessel slowly sailed out of the harbor into the open sea, carrying two hundred and eleven refugees. They had in very truth, forsaken all and followed Christ. Many of them were in rags, their garments having been worn out by contact with the briers and underbrush of the mountains. All were without money; for the current proverb, "No law for Calvinists," had been followed to its last extremity by their Roman Catholic debtors and kinsfolk. But it was the universal testimony that no word of complaint escaped them. On the contrary, hymns of praise and prayers to Heaven for their persecutors, who "knew not what they did," rose constantly from the midst of the little band.

One of the passengers, who observed them, exclaimed: "If I were called upon to choose a religion suddenly and without further thought, I should fix upon that of these people, because they suffer so uncomplainingly."

Their course lay in the direction of Trinidad, the island in the mouth of the Orinoco, under the dominion of Great Britain. The passage of the two hundred and eleven exiles was arranged for by British planters, who were then in great need of laborers on their sugar plantations; but the natural explanation removes none of the impressiveness of a divine interposition at a time when people are in great extremity. Dr. Kalley's faith was honored, and the simple-hearted people's prayers for deliverance were answered—the English ships had come!

In Trinidad was a strange mixture of races, and the Roman Catholic was still

the dominant religion; but there was at
least freedom of worship guaranteed to
the Protestant Portuguese by the English
occupancy of the island.   Here also came
Mr. Hewitson, who was sent among them
to reorganize the Church, which had, of
course, lost its early organic form.   Other
exiles were constantly arriving, their pass-
ports having been granted by the civil
authorities of Funchal, who were persuaded to avail themselves of this oppor-
tunity to rid the island of the trouble-
some heretics.

The number who thus left Madeira was
in the neighborhood of one thousand persons, and that the very best blood of the
country; but the bishop proclaimed a
solemn assembly in the churches, and ordered the Te Deum sung in thanksgiving
that "the wolves" had been providen-
tially cast out of the fold.

Mr. Hewitson's impaired health permitted him to remain but two months, and in his stead came Mr. Da Silva, a native-born pastor, with newly-received orders from the Free Church of Scotland.

Mr. Da Silva was the possessor of great inherited wealth, and was of high social standing in Funchal. His daughter was the wife of a judge, and the influence of his son-in-law for a considerable time protected him from the more violent persecutions; but at last he, too, was compelled to flee for his life, leaving his wife, child, home, and fortune forever.

When his name, as pastor, was first suggested to the congregation in Trinidad, the people were asked to raise their hands in approval, and it is said the entire congregation instantly rose as one man, and extended their hands as high as they could. He was received with demonstrations of great joy by the little company of his fellow-sufferers; but it was a hard field of. labor, extending some twelve or fourteen miles inland, and embracing some smaller islands lying about Trinidad. There was a deep personal note in the relation of pastor and people, and it is related that every morning Mr. Da Silva would make the circuit of his parishioners' homes near by, knock at the doors, and call them to a morning praise service before attending to the duties of the day.

The climate of Trinidad was very trying upon the Portuguese, unaccustomed to such extreme heat, and the necessity of working in the midst of the irrigating ditches of the sugar plantations brought on malarial fever. Hundreds died from the exposure, and in the comparatively healthful locality of the capital, Port of Spain, there were but precarious means of gaining a livelihood.

The sufferings of the people were very

6

great, and, as there was no chance of obtaining freeholds, it was determined that they emigrate to the United States. The people had earned the means for the payment of their own passage to New York, and once there, were aided as it became necessary by the American Protestant Society. Here their pastor, Mr. Da Silva, who had preceded the greater part of his flock, and made the voyage in great feebleness of body, rapidly grew worse. The dying words of the Prince of Orange were, "God pity this poor people," and even so the burden of this faithful man of God's thought was ever of his scattered and persecuted brethren.

But it was not permitted for him to pass over into their promised land with them, and on one of the bitterly cold days of that trying winter of 1848 he was laid to rest. The American friends who gathered in the church that day to pay a last respect to the dead were moved to tears as the whole body of homeless, friendless exiles rose in their seats and united their voices in a tremulous song of their native tongue.

In October of the following year, in response to an invitation from a committee, including the governor of the State, the exiles came to Illinois, and settled permanently, part of them in Springfield, and the rest in Jacksonville. One other settlement was also formed, but later was abandoned. In 1850 a native pastor was installed over the Churches, sent out by the Free Church of Scotland, and for three years supported by that body. Dr. Kalley came later, and for a brief time resided with the converts, and assisted in the ministry of the regular pastor.

As evidence of the integrity of the original company of Portuguese, it is related that a number of them, as they became able, desired to purchase permanent homes on the outskirts of Jacksonville. One of the number was selected to attend to the business details, and he secured a tract of land containing fifty-five acres, which was to be divided among some ten or more men. Each of the number made his payment for one, two, three, or five acres, as they severally desired, and gave it into the hands of their chosen representative. He gathered the money together—it was all in coin—and, carrying it in a wicker basket brought from the old country, made the entire payment, and received a deed made out to him alone. In the course of time he gave to each man his separate deed; but there was no hurry about it, there had never been a scrap of paper either asked or given in acknowledgment of the funds he held in trust. They believed in one another, these pure-hearted people who had lived through perilous times, facing death and danger together. And the truth had penetrated their inner life so very deeply that they conformed their habits to its severe and simple teachings, and followed out Paul's charge to "lead quiet and peaceable lives in all godliness and honesty."

They were a home-loving, unaffected people, and reflected the nobler qualities of the Portuguese race, coming as they did from the sturdy middle class, which contains the source of strength in all countries. Their wants were few and easily attained, and the peasant virtues of frugality and industry are their marked characteristics.

Their men were brave soldiers, and fought during our Civil War as faithfully for the Union as did any native-born patriots. The captain of one Illinois company bore testimony to the soldierly qualities of the Portuguese men who served under him by declaring that if he ever went to war again he would prefer to lead a company composed strictly of Portuguese.

They love our flag, they rejoice in the freedom it stands for; and in view of all they have suffered at the hands of the Roman Catholic Church, it is perhaps not to be wondered at that these survivors of the persecutions of Madeira fear the presence of this power within our borders as the visible token, not only of all that is most intolerant in human creeds, but of all that is subversive of the principles of human justice in governments.

For almost fifty years this transplanted people has given allegiance to our Government, accepting its freedom, and honoring its laws; though they have dwelt apart, preserving their speech, and holding to the habits of the old country. But no people, save the Hebrew, can ever hope perfectly to maintain a race barrier, and as the original exiles have been passing away, the new generations that have risen to take their places are Americans.

The circumstances under which the fathers came, expatriated them so thoroughly that they could hand down to their children no love of their own native country. The language is dying out, and English is beginning to be spoken in the Church services. American sons have found the Portuguese daughters "fair to look upon," and within another half century the absorption into the stronger English race will be complete, and only the beautiful story of the exiles from Madeira will remain among us.

Chapter IV.

MISSIONS IN NEW LANDS.

ONCE more glancing backward to the history of the mother country, we find the Portuguese sailors continuing their search for the sea route to the Indies. In 1497, Vasco Da Gama doubled the Cape of Good Hope, and reached India by sea; and that event marks the entrance upon the heroic age of Portuguese history. The fifteenth century will always be characterized by historians as an age of unrest. While Charles the Fifth was fighting the awakening spirit of civil and religious liberty in his Dutch provinces, and England was in the perilous hours preceding the birth of the Reformation, and France was quenching the life of the new faith, Portugal was at

HAMMOCK BORNE BY PORTERS.

rest from these internal dissensions. It is true the Inquisition was established within her borders; but the new faith had made slight progress among the conservative Portuguese, and the awakening energies of the race found an outlet in the enterprises of the far East.

The adventurers penetrated into China and Japan. Settlements were formed in both these countries, in India, and the outlying islands of the South Pacific. These settlements required the protection of military force, and during that eventful century Portugal sent the best blood of the nation to maintain her supremacy.

The story of this forcible occupation of India reads like a romance, and the wild dream of Portugal that she would some day establish a powerful empire in the East, which would eventually absorb all the other Oriental powers, seems not altogether impossible of fulfillment in view of what the little nation actually did accomplish.

The commercial power of Venice was transferred to Lisbon, which now became the great entrepôt for the Eastern products. Merchants from all over Europe came to Lisbon to lay in their stocks of spices from the Spice Islands, the pepper of the Malabar coast, the teas and silks of China, the calicoes of Calicut, and the muslins of Bengal. The king of Portugal was known as the richest sovereign in Christendom, and alliances with the reigning house were eagerly sought by the noblest families of Europe. Lisbon was the greatest commercial center of the world.

In one of the earlier expeditions toward the East, conducted by Pedro Alvares Cabral, he was driven by stress of weather towards the open western seas. Thus, by chance, he discovered what is now known as Brazil. As it contained no established empire, and seemed a country fitted only for agricultural purposes, it was not considered an acquisition of much importance. The first settlers were convicts and abandoned women, forcibly deported from Portugal; but later the peasants in large numbers sought homes there, and before the end of the fifteenth century, Brazil had become a flourishing dependency of the Portuguese power.

Portugal had risen slowly to her proud eminence among the nations of Europe, and her prosperity contained the seeds of her decay. It is the old and oft-repeated story of luxury enervating the forces of a nation. Then, too, the colonization of Brazil, of various points on the African coast, of Madeira, the Azores, Mozambique, of strategic points in India, of the islands of the East Indies, and

of points in China and Japan had necessarily exhausted her vitality. Embroil-
ing herself with European quarrels, the
enterprising and more practical Dutch
had stolen a march on her, and were fast
absorbing the Eastern trade. They went
to the Orient as private speculators in
their own ships, caring nothing for dominion, and requiring no costly armies
to sustain them. In the end they con-
quered by the superior strength of Dutch
persistence, and Portugal's dream of empire in the East was over. Then, in
1578 came the news of the death of Dom
Sebastian and of the destruction of his
army. There was not a noble family in
Portugal but mourned the loss of one or
more representatives in that stricken
army of young Crusaders, and there was
not a loyal citizen in the kingdom but
knew the glory of Portugal had departed.
The alarm reached to India, and the brave

old viceroy died of a broken heart at the news.

In less than four years, Portugal was a dependency of the Spanish crown, and was entering upon that mournful period of her history known as the "Sixty Years' Captivity." At the end of that time she succeeded in throwing off the hated Castilian yoke, but it was as one of the minor and insignificant powers of Europe she came into her own again. In past glory alone she is great. And through all these years Brazil was expanding into a vigorous young country, with a teeming population.

It was to this people of the Portuguese tongue that Dr. Kalley, in the early fifties, directed his later energies. His wife having died some years previous, the doctor spent some time in travel, after he had been compelled to abandon Madeira. While in Palestine, he had been called to

attend upon a gentleman who was seek-
ing restoration to health in that mild
climate. His daughter was accompanying the invalid, and this lady, whom he
met in this way, afterward became the
wife of Dr. Kalley.

Later, the doctor joined the settlement
in Illinois, and for a year dwelt among
these people of his first ministry, assist-
ing the native-born pastor in his duties,
and sustaining a relation to the people
that was rather paternal than anything
else.

A question had arisen among the
Churches in regard to the validity of the
Romish baptism. Dr. Kalley, after long
and serious thought upon the subject,
gave it as his opinion that, inasmuch as
the Romish Church had so far departed
from the simplicity of faith, and as the
priesthood was a corrupt priesthood, it
was better for the converts from the an-

cient Church to be rebaptized. Trivial
as the question now seems, and of no importance ever but to a single generation
of men, it created much discussion, and
finally resulted in a division of the
Church—one body holding to the opinion
that the Romish baptism was sufficient,
and the other body insisting upon the re-
baptism of an applicant before being ad-
mitted to membership. The rupture
grieved Dr. Kalley, and he at once discontinued his ministry among the people,
and sailed for Brazil, once more bound
upon an independent mission. Estab-
lishing himself in Rio Janeiro, he began
work with much the same methods which
had borne such fruit in Madeira.

It was a new and unworked mission-
field, and as definite results began to appear, the hostility of the Romanists was
aroused, and the attention of the Government was directed towards the infant

mission.   In a Privy Council of the empire, the matter of expelling Dr. Kalley
from Brazil was argued, the emperor himself bearing a part in the discussion.

Dom Pedro was a broad-minded, liberal
man, who had at heart the real interests
of his subjects, and who made himself
personally conversant with the affairs of
the empire.   He was, in many respects,
the first Brazilian of his time.   One who
was personally acquainted with them all,
compared the four emperors—the French,
the Austrian, the Russian, and Brazilian—and affirmed that Dom Pedro was
the superior of the four.   Though a Romanist himself, he was not a bigot.   Perhaps his Italian empress and his German
mother had helped to widen his sympa-
thies, as his love of learning had certainly enlarged his mental vision.   It is
said it was a custom of his to entertain,
in his official residence of São Christovão,

travelers coming from foreign countries, that he might study their various languages and become familiar with their customs.

He had interested himself in the Scotch missionary, and had even called upon him in person. It was doubtless due to the influence of the emperor that it was decided, in the Privy Council, Dr. Kalley might remain and pursue his work.

The Brazilians have not that nobility of character found among the Portuguese. They are more given to the baser vices of mankind, and are more indifferent to civilizing influences; but they have the inquiring disposition that leads them to listen to the presentation of new truths. They are fond of argument, always desiring to hear both sides well and fairly given.

But they were not so responsive as their kinsmen of the older country.

Even the adherents of the established religion were not so firm in their attachment. A spirit of irreligion which is harder to overcome than pronounced opposition was abroad in the land. This indifference was especially marked among the Brazilian men. "We leave that to the women," they would answer lightly when approached upon the subject of religion. And so the work progressed much more slowly than it had done in Madeira, because of this inherent difference in the two peoples of a common stock.

Dr. Kalley's second wife was a lady of large fortune, and her heart was fully in her husband's work; and, true to his early idea, the doctor organized his work upon a self-supporting basis.

In Madeira, the source of his power had been his medical skill, which has ever been the missionary's most effective human weapon; but in Brazil it was even

a disadvantage to him. The native physicians, though not well qualified in the
profession, were extremely jealous of all
foreign doctors, and, adapting himself to
the altered conditions, Dr. Kalley made
no attempt to extend his practice beyond
the converts he soon organized into a
Church.

This Church, built of Dr. Kalley's mu-
nificence, in cosmopolitan Rio Janeiro,
became the center of a new life, that was
to engraft itself upon the decaying body
of Roman Catholic Brazil. Dr. Kalley
taught and trained his converts after the
manner of the early Church fathers, and
insisted upon correct living as the necessary outcome of true believing.

The priests had so thoroughly in-
structed the people in the devious wind-
ings of mental reservations, and the ad-
visability of lying when the object to be
gained was a good one, that the psalmist

might have said of the Brazilians, without any after-confession of haste, "All men are liars." Dr. Kalley's followers were distinctively known as persons who spoke the severe and simple truth, and it has since passed into a proverb in Brazil that the word of a Protestant needs no bond to support it.

There was no Sabbath in the land. Saints' days were observed until after the morning mass; but the Lord's day passed like any other ordinary day of the busy week.

Dr. Kalley's followers were further distinguished as Sabbath observers. One of the converts was a native of Portugal, who had engaged in the manufacture of hats in a humble way. The probability was that his business would suffer by shutting down on Sunday; but he did not hesitate to keep the day of rest because of that. A brother, who was a priest in Portugal, had some money invested in the enterprise, and when he was informed of the proposed change, wrote back: "I care not whether you keep open or closed on Sunday, only let me be assured my money is safe." .

It is a strange fact that after the hatter's conversion and subsequent observance of the Sabbath, his business grew from its humble beginnings into great proportions. He was the winner of one of the gold medals in our Centennial Exposition at Philadelphia, and became one of the wealthy men of Rio Janeiro, his consecration keeping pace with the increase of his worldly possessions. His gift of ten thousand dollars, with Dr. Kalley's gift of a like sum, made possible the building of a forty thousand-dollar church in the city when the mission had grown into permanency. This increase in material prosperity is so frequently

marked in mission-fields that, beyond the
fact that clean living and right thinking
give to persons an added mental and
physical vigor in whatever calling in life
they pursue, there does seem to be something very like the operation of the ancient law which brought prosperity to a
Hebrew in proportion to the righteous-
ness of his life.

The same increase in individual cases
might be more obvious among us of the
enlightened people if men regulated their
lives by the austere precepts of the gospel as does a newly-converted heathen,
who is opening his mind and heart, like
a thirsty flower lifting its chalice to the
down-falling of a beneficent rain, to a direct revelation from the Most High, which
he has never even heard mention of in all
his life up to that wonderful moment.
When one hears the Truth like that, be-

lieving, it is ample compensation for having been born a heathen.

With Dr. Kalley were associated a number of Bible-readers, whose duties were to visit from house to house. He supported these men and their families from his own private purse. A Church was founded in the city of Rio Grande, across the bay from Rio Janeiro, and another one in Pernambuco. These three Churches were Presbyterian in spirit and doctrine, though never actually identified with the Church at large. Dr. Kalley's wealth largely supported them all; but in time they became self-supporting.

During their residence in Rio Janeiro the doctor and his wife adopted a boy, whom they educated. He has been for many years engaged in evangelizing among the Jews, though he himself is not of that race.

Dr. Kalley personally served the Church in the great capital city of the empire for more than twenty years, but failing strength and advancing years at last compelled his retirement from the work he loved so well. As his successor in Rio Janeiro he named a young man whom he had personally trained and sent back to London for a three years' course in Spurgeon's Pastors' College. Breathing the spirit of his devoted missionary father, and of the famous London divine as well, he has proved himself a worthy successor in this natural center of a great and fast-spreading mission.

In his old home in Edinburgh, Dr. Kalley passed the remainder of his days; and when the news of his death was carried across the water, there was sorrow in many lands, and tears—such tears as never fall save for the loss of some high-souled man who has loved his fellow-men

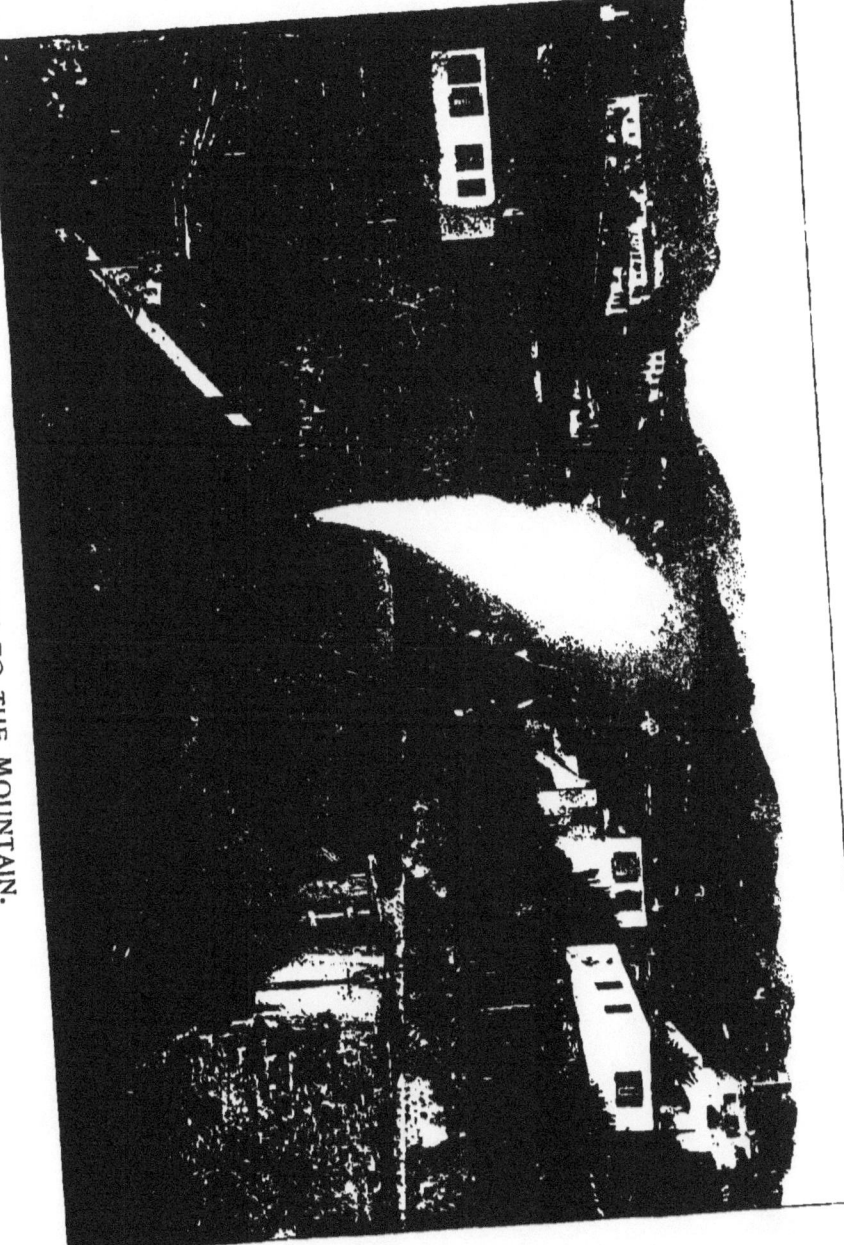

RAILROAD TRAIN TO THE MOUNTAIN.

with a deep and self-abnegating love, and has given the strength of his years to lift them nearer Christ.

He was buried in his beloved Scotland. A simple stone of Scotch granite marks his resting-place, and it bears this faithful record

" Till He comes,
in
Tender and reverent memory of
ROBERT REID KALLEY, M. D.
Born Sep. 8th, 1809.
Fell asleep, Jan. 17th, 1888.
A servant of God
in
Madeira, Brazil, and other lands.

His delight was in the law of the Lord, and in His law did he meditate day and night; whose faith follow, considering the end of his conversation in

JESUS CHRIST,
The same yesterday, to-day, and forever."

Moved by a desire permanently to preserve some expression of their love and gratitude, the Brazilians caused an inscribed tablet to be placed in the wall of the church at the right of the tomb, and upon the left is a similar mural tablet, presented by the Illinois Churches, which bears this insciption:

"To the beloved and honored memory
of
Their father in the gospel,
DR. KALLEY;
From the Churches of the
Madeirenses
'Scattered abroad'
in 1846:
By Romish persecution,
1838 to 1883.
'The name of the Lord Jesus Christ was magnified.'"

Chapter V.

IN BRAZIL.

IT may be said of Dr. Kalley that he was the pioneer of missionaries in Brazil. The Presbyterian Church later occuped the field which his individual enterprise had opened. Six Presbyteries under one general and independent Synod now cover the territory in which are nearly fifteen million souls, the Presbyterian Chuch, South, supporting its own missionaries, the Presbyterian Church supporting the ones to whom that body has given authority,—all working harmoniously in one great, common cause.

The main entering wedge in Brazil has been the educational facilities afforded by the Church of the missionaries.

A school was founded in Rio Janeiro;

but the unhealthfulness of that city during certain months in the year compelled
its removal to the city of São Paulo,
three hundred miles southwest of the
capital, in the salubrious, mountainous
part of the province of São Paulo. Five
hundred students are in attendance. The
work is mainly for the training of native
ministers and teachers; but all depart-
ments of instruction, even to kindergar-
ten, are equipped.

During the reign of Dom Pedro, the
emperor and his suite made a visit of
inspection. After he had carefully inquired into the course of instruction, and
had been conducted through the institu-
tion, he exclaimed with delight, in the
presence of his ministers, " There is nothing like it in the empire."

This visit of the great man is still remembered by the missionary teachers,
who, though aliens themselves, shared in

the general enthusiasm as Dom Pedro rode through the streets, bowing to right and left, his fine face wearing a smile as he caught the acclamations of his loyal and delighted subjects. But even then there was a strong undercurrent of feeling throughout the empire against the perpetuation of the monarchy, that found expression in a muttered discontent whenever the haughty figure of Dom Pedro's son-in-law, who had not the grace even to incline his head in acknowledgment of the salutations of the Brazilians, appeared in the presence of the people. Even upon that day, in São Paulo, there was a passing and suppressed whisper of, "Wait until Dom Pedro's day is over; then we shall see whether a Jesuit shall rule the empire."

The school at São Paulo brought the missionaries in contact with a higher order of people than are usually accessible

to foreigners.   Among them was a bar-
oness, the members of whose family have
ever since been influential workers in the
São Paulo Church.   Through the kinder-
garten teacher, who was a woman of rare
graces, the grandchildren of a senator,
wealthy and of a noble house, were
reached.   The senator himself was advanced in years, and, while he did not
become a believer, gave his consent to his
family accepting the new faith.

"I am too old to change," he said,
"and prefer to die in the bosom of my
Church."   But a few years later, no less
than twenty members of his family had
united with the Church.

There have been some five or six
priests to renounce their faith.   One of
them seems to have been a man of singu-
lar nobility of character.   When he began
his studies for the priesthood, a relative,
who by some chance had become pos-

sessed of a Bible, gave it to the young
man, thinking it would be of more use to
a priest than to him. It was not a book,
however, to which much importance was
attached in his course of instruction.
There were books on theology, many and
various, and books concerning the institu-
tions, the doctrines, and ceremonies of the
Church, but not much of the Bible in any
of them.

He read, and perceived the wide di-
vergence of his Church from the spirit of
the early Church of the apostles, and
then began a struggle which lasted for
eighteen years. He entered upon the
work for which he had fitted and fulfilled
his priestly duties ; but he afterward said,
"I knew I was preaching lies whenever I
stood before my people."

Over his diocese was a bishop who had
a conscience, too. They often talked
over the matter which was troubling the

heart of the younger man, and once the priest daringly preached for two hours in the presence of his ecclesiastical superior. It was an unmistakably genuine and fervent gospel sermon ; but the bishop only listened and held his peace, not even reprimanding him privately. There was something in the close fraternal relations of these two which was very much like the sentiment holding Luther, during the years of his doubt, to Staupitz. Finally the long and agonizing conflict ended in the priest's withdrawal from the Roman Catholic Church, and his union with the Church of the Presbyterian missionaries.

He became a minister, and organized a Church of seventy members in the town of Brotas, in which he had been for so many years a priest. His blameless life, and the eloquence with which he proclaimed the gospel, made him a power in the Church. His converts caught his zeal. Two brothers, who had been re-claimed from Romanism by him, made a journey of two hundred miles that a third brother, who lived in the mining district, might also become a partaker of the faith. He was converted during the visit, and a Church of fourteen members, which con-sisted of his own family alone, was organ-ized.

In the vicinity of Brotas there lived a man who was the terror of his part of the country. He was a man of powerful frame and great strength, and was of so quar-relsome a disposition that his neighbors shunned him and fled at his approach. He always carried a huge dirk in his belt, and in one of his encounters had killed a man. But remorse sometimes visited him, and during one of these times of mental agony he called a servant, and sent him with a cow to the parish priest.

"Tell the father," he said, "to say as

8

many masses for my soul as the value of the cow.   I must have peace."

The holy father accepted the cow, and said the masses—perhaps.   But the man received no answering peace, and at last, in despair, ordered his horse, and rode towards the house of a neighbor, one of the brothers who were of the ex-priest's recent converts.   Some one had told him of a new book which this man had, that seemed to have a strange power in quieting the passions and fears of a human heart.

In considerable fear and hesitation the master of the house advanced to meet his guest, and with surprise learned of his wish to hear the Bible read.   He turned to the Book of John, and read about "the light that shineth in darkness," and read on until dinner-time.   After dinner he read until evening, and then his self-invited guest left, saying:

"I want my wife to hear about this."

The next day he brought her with him, and the reading continued steadily for several days, when the long-desired peace came—the "light that shineth in darkness." The whole character of the man was changed. From being the terror of the neighborhood, he became a peacemaker, to whose arbitration other people brought their wordy battles.

One of the first acts that he performed after the confession of his faith was the freeing of all his slaves. He had never learned to read; but he procured a Bible, and marked, in a way in which he could distinguish them, the passages in which he especially delighted. That Bible was his constant companion. In the market, along the road, or wherever he hailed people, he would stop and ask them to listen, while he opened his Bible, and repeated from memory the marked passages.

But the ex-priest, who ministered to the little flock, was made to feel the unfriendliness of his old, forsaken Church, and it was thought wisest for him to visit from place to place as a sort of traveling evangelist. He was a perfect flame of zeal, winning men by the compassionate, divine love that dwelt in him, though he was a man of winning personality aside from that. But the spirit of such men consumes the vital forces of the body quickly, as a candle burning in a breeze, and there came a day when he felt his strength was going.

It so happened that in his journey he drew near a Government hospital. He entered, and asked if he might rest, and the major in command of the hospital gave him permission. He held some conversation with this major, who was a man high in civil authority and of considerable wealth, and gave him the pocket

Bible and hymn-book which had been his faithful companions during the years of a weary pilgrimage. And then he died— died as fearlessly as he had lived. The major gave orders that he receive a Christian burial; and, thinking he must have been a faithful son of the Church, the parish priest buried him in consecrated ground, with the rites of the Roman Catholic Church.

Before many days there was a great stir, and the news was spread abroad that a heretic lay in the shadow of the church. The parish priest, in great wrath, went directly to the major, and said:

"Why did you order me to give that man a Christian burial, knowing, as you did, that he was a heretic?"

"I ordered him to recieve a Christian burial," responded the major, "because he was a Christian—a better Christian than ever you or I have been."

"You shall be excommunicated for this," threatened the priest.

"I am excommunicated already," replied the major. "I have excommunicated myself. Here is my religion," and he took from his breast-pocket the little Bible which had been given him.

A guard of soldiers were stationed about the grave to prevent the Romanists from dishonoring the remains, which were afterward disinterred, and given a peaceful rest in a Protestant burying-ground.

The major openly avowed his faith. He and his family became earnest workers in the Church of the missionaries.

It is said that when the bishop, who had been so familiarly acquainted with the ex-priest, came to die, he seemed to be in great distress. Calling a priest to his bedside, he said:

"Can you not call upon some saint of

your devotion to intercede for me? It
goes evil with me—it goes evil with me!"
And thus he died.

There was another class of people to
come under the influence of the missionaries. These were the Negroes, who,
during the long occupancy of Brazil as
missionary territory, from their condition
of servitude, were being gradually eman-
cipated by the operation of the decree of
1871. Against them, as a race, there was
not found among the Brazilians that in-
eradicable prejudice that exists among us
towards the freedmen.

It is but scant justice to allow that the
history of the Roman Catholic Church
shows that, wherever that Church has
been dominant, there has never been so
sharp a distinction between bond and
free. In the thought of the Church, their
souls are of equal value; and, in point of
fact, both are in spiritual servitude to an

aristocracy which is none the less preten-
tious and powerful because its ranks are
filled by men who come from every
class—from ancient and opulent houses
of the nobility, and from among the
meanest born in the lowliest walks of
life as well.   It is affirmed, too, that the
Brazilian Negroes, as a rule, are of a
somewhat higher order of men than have
been held in slavery elsewhere, of greater
strength and stature, of better and more
regular features, and of greater mental
vigor.

In the Churches, they have been ad-
mitted in exactly the same standing with
their white brethren, and no protest has
ever been made.

In the town of Viera fully one-half
the population are Negroes, and more
than one-half the members of the mission Church are of the same blood.   The
minister, at one time in charge of the

work in that place, had in his service a young Negro who had lately been converted. He was almost twenty-one years old, and of powerful physique; but one day he said to the minister:

"My mother beats me because I come to your church."

"That is hard to bear," said the minister; "but it is one of the trials of your Christian faith. Show your mother obedience in everything she asks of you except the giving up of your religion, and I will pray that her heart may be softened."

The young fellow's life was so consistent that, after a time, his mother felt a curiosity to know what strange power it was that gave him strength to resist her, and yet with patience to endure the floggings. She went with him to Church. The minister did not denounce her Church, or say one word concerning its false teachings.

"I only preached Jesus," he said.

After the sermon, he walked down, and shook her hand.

"How did you like it?" he asked.

"That was good," she said, "and I want to hear more."

She heard more, and in a few weeks became a Christian.

There is a third class which, on account of the great press of work and because the laborers are so sadly few, have scarcely been touched. These are the Indians, the aboriginals of Brazil, who have been crowded outside the limits of civilization, much as they have been with us. During Dom Pedro's time, with his characteristic benevolence, he had Government teachers employed for them; but after the fall of the empire, these educating agencies were withdrawn.

Under the empire, Church and State were united, and the priests were sustained out of the national treasury. There was little of the ancient evangelizing spirit among the profligate body; but after teachers were appointed, the priests occasionally visited the Indians. The teachers appealed to the emperor, praying that these priests be forbidden to visit among their wards, because they taught them gambling and all manner of immorality.

One of the missionaries tells of his attempt to start a mission among some of the southern tribes; but the change in the Government was made soon after, and he adds sorrowfully, "And I had to leave my poor Indians."

The Brazilians have an instinctive love for a theoretical free government, but practically they are not yet equal to sustaining one with credit. But the change from an hereditary monarchy was a propitious one for the missionary work.

Dom Pedro's tolerance was not one of the graces of his daughter or her French consort, who stood next in the order of succession. Both were under Jesuit in-' fluence, and were narrow Romanists, and had they been permitted to pursue their own political course, it would have fared ill with the fast-growing missions.

By the change in Government, Church and State were divorced, and the State funds could no longer be diverted to the support of the Roman Catholic Church. That has quickened the activity of the priests, and, while there never has been real persecution in Brazil, the Church is striving to regain and hold its old su- premacy as never before.

The hope of the Republic lies, in no small degree, with the extension and vi- tality of Protestant educational mission- work within the borders of Brazil. That there is a crying need for the moral re-

generation of this Portuguese-speaking
people, and for the presence of a pure
faith among them, is fully illustrated by
the case of a young man who had applied
for membership in the Presbyterian
Church in Rio Janeiro. He had made a
satisfactory confession of faith, and answered the questions put to him until
they asked:

"Do you keep the Seventh Command-
ment?"

"Do you think," he exclaimed, "there
is a young man in all Brazil who does
observe that?"

He was, of course, rejected; but it
stands in evidence of the widespread cor-
ruption in a country where the Roman
Catholic clergy hold the consciences of
the people and the absolving power over
their sins.

Chapter VI.

A WIDENING FIELD.

ONCE more returning to the exiles from Madeira, it seems that with such a history behind them, and holding the memory of their great and good missionary father so sacredly, the Churches of the Illinois settlements could never have been otherwise than deeply filled with the missionary spirit. They themselves, as a Church, were the result of missionary enterprise, and their hearts instinctively turned to others of their race dwelling in spiritual darkness.

The modern Portuguese is distinguished by the adventurous spirit much as were his cavalier ancestors of the fifteenth and sixteenth centuries, and the hardy sons of Madeira and the Continent

are found in various portions of the world,
living in communities of their own people, preserving their customs, and speak-
ing their native language. In Massachusetts and along the New England coast,
they are found in large numbers. In California, and stretching northward to the
farthest limits of Washington, are yet
other large colonies.

In the Hawaiian Islands, one-sixth of
the population are Portuguese. They are
at work mainly upon the sugar plantations, numbers of them having remained
since the early whaling times, when from
three to four hundred whaling-vessels an-
nually visited the islands. They are gen-
erally by the sea. They love its keen,
salt breeze, and the eternal murmur of its
waters.

They are Roman Catholics almost to a
man, and the efforts of the humble little
colony in the heart of Illinois have been

especially directed toward all of these waiting fields.

Three men and their wives followed Dr. Kalley, to assist in opening up the work in Brazil; later, six others were sent out. Two are laboring in California, two in Massachusetts, and two have gone to Portugal. Five have gone to Madeira, which is now a comparatively safe field of work, made so by the Christian sentiment of the world recoiling against persecution.

In 1890 the mission to the Hawaiian Islands was inaugurated by a minister who came as a boy with the original band of exiles. He was educated for the ministry, was for three years a missionary in Brazil, and has served as pastor among his countrymen in the Illinois Churches for twenty-six years. Some years after the Civil War he visited Madeira, and preached to a gathering of neighbors in the house of a kinsman.

It had been his birthplace, and the home from which his family had fled for their lives because of the same gospel he proclaimed in security that day. And now, as this "Story of Madeira" draws to a close, there comes the news of his sudden taking out of life. He was one of the fast disappearing links that bind the people to the time of the persecution.

There was a strength and vigor in the character of that earlier generation not found in this. Among them all, none possessed more fully the distinguishing marks of that generation of Christians, and none possessed the broad culture and gift of leadership which gave to Rev. E. N. Pires among his own people the place left vacant by the death of Dr. Kalley. There was ever apparent in him this thought, that the ministry to which he had been called was pre-eminently a high calling among men. He fully real-

9

ized in his own life and character the dignity of that calling, and the wide and tender charity for which it stands. Two years ago he gave his young daughter to the Hawaiian work. With her have been associated six others.

Hardly to be classified as an outgrowth of Dr. Kalley's work, and yet most intimately associated with it, is the life-labor of a man who was not born of the Portuguese race.

Away back in the early fifties he was a student in an Eastern college. He was chosen to take part in an open literary meeting, and debate upon some question involving the political history of North and South America. He prepared to speak upon his side of the question; but from some cause was unable to appear. So slight a cause as that was sufficient to turn the current of a life. From his researches he became strangely interested

in the Brazilians, and came to feel he had
received a direct summons to missionary
work among them.   By the time he had
completed his course, the Civil War opening prevented his being sent just then
by the Presbyterian Board of Missions.
But the Madeira exiles had already settled in their new home in Illinois, and
a call was made for a pastor, as the native
pastor was not equal to the work of the
several Churches.

Impressed that this was a providential
opening for him to master the Portuguese
language, acquaint himself with the people, and prepare for a wider field, the
young minister responded to the call, and
was installed as pastor over two of the
Churches.   Later, he labored in Brazil
for many years, and has given two sons
and two daughters to the work in that
field.

And there is a personal history behind

each one of these thirty-seven names of those who have gone out from this single Illinois colony to do missionary work, some of them most touching and of deep interest. Some young and high ambitions have been laid in sacrifice upon the altar, the closest and tenderest of human ties broken, and, in some cases, years of slow toil, in the midst of poverty, have been spent in fitting for work. The list given, containing the thirty-seven names and their respective fields of labor, closes with this pathetic little line: "Others willing to go if they only had the means."

Bishop Taylor writes thus of Dr. Kalley's life and mission: "All this illustrates the vitality of hardy, self-supporting missions. They can be 'scattered abroad;' but every fragment sticks where it strikes, and takes root, and grows, and produces fruit to the glory of God."

And, indeed, no more marvelous widen-

ing of one man's pure devotion has the
world ever beheld, from the moment that
a young man of twenty-nine years of age,
possessed of every gift that makes life
full and rich, stood on the deck of an
ocean steamer and listened while God
called—called through a human affliction.
A thousand converts on a single island,
a whole Christianized people, transplanted to a distant land, there to per-
petuate their race and faith, and a mighty
missionary influence that is not ended,
but only gathering force as the years
go by.

Ended—nay! not until the sower and
the reaper shall rejoice together and unite
their voices in one grand, triumphant,
"Harvest Home."

HILDEBRAND AND CICELY;
Or, The Monk of Tavystoke Abbaye.

By M. A. PAULL.

12mo.   Cloth.   One illustration.   359 pages, ... *$1.00.*

"Not every sweet Cicely of those dark ages found so generous and loyal a confessor as heroic Hildebrand; not every monk so fully kept the sacred vows of his order. The language is chaste, the style attractive. . . . As a study of that eventful period, just at the dawn of the Reformation, and of the monastic life which was so potent a factor in it, the book is of great value."—*Christian Advocate, Syracuse, N. Y.*

GRANDMONT:
Stories of an Old Monastery.

By HON. WALTER T. GRIFFIN.

12mo.   Cloth.   Illustrated.   272 pages, ... *$1.20.*

"It is not so much a romance as a series of romantic incidents, drawn from the veritable history of one of the most celebrated religious establishments of mediæval France. . . . The character of the pious Abbot Etienne, who exhibits the mind of Christ in an age of rudeness, cruelty, greed, and superstition, and the exploits of the giant monk, Hugues, whose memory still lives in the traditions of the French peasantry, are the most notable features of a book which is entertaining and instructive to a remarkable degree."—*Sunday-school Journal, New York.*

CURTS & JENNINGS, Cincinnati, Chicago, St. Louis.

THE LEAST OF THESE:
And Other Stories.

By L. T. MEADE.

12mo. Cloth. Illustrated. 250 pages, ... 75 cents.

"The writer has a tender spot in his heart for children, and his pictures of child-life in the slums of the great cities is intensely realistic."—*Christian Observer*.

"The book is distinguished by deep, intelligent character study and strong examples of the helpfulness of the gospel to the most lowly."—*Young Men's Era*.

NATURE AS A BOOK OF SYMBOLS.

By WM. MARSHALL.

12mo. Cloth. 277 pages, ... 90 cents.

"The work is thoughtful, philosophical, and logical, and is replete with food for profitable reflection. It demonstrates the absurdity of both the atheistic and agnostic theories of creation, and annihilates the excuses commonly urged by unbelief."—*Religious Telescope*.

"The mind is certainly dull that can not find both pleasure and profit from these pages. To the sermon-builder they will suggest both methods and material for the forceful illustration of truth, while to the thoughtful layman, old or young, they will reveal new realms of beauty in the ever-open book of nature."—*Methodist Herald*.

CURTS & JENNINGS, Cincinnati, Chicago, St. Louis.